CAMP JUPITER CLASSIFIED

A PROBATIO'S JOURNAL

 • HYPERION

Los Angeles   New York

AN OFFICIAL RICK RIORDAN COMPANION BOOK

A special thank-you to Stephanie True Peters
for her help with this book

Illustrations by Stefanie Masciandaro
Map illustrations by John S. Dykes

First Edition, May 2020
1 3 5 7 9 10 8 6 4 2
FAC-020093-20080
Printed in the United States of America

This book is set in Times New Roman/Fontspring
Designed by Joann Hill and Shelby Kahr

Library of Congress Cataloging-in-Publication Data
Names: Riordan, Rick, author. Title: Camp Jupiter
classified: a probatio's journal / Rick Riordan.
Description: First edition. • Los Angeles : Disney-Hyperion, 2020. •
"An official Rick Riordan companion book." • Audience: Ages 8–12. •
Audience: Grades 4–6. • Summary: "When mysterious incidents start
wreaking havoc throughout Camp Jupiter, suspicion falls on the Fourth
Cohort's newest probatio. But is she really to blame? Find out the truth by
delving into the pages of her personal journal"—Provided by publisher.
Identifiers: LCCN 2019041794 • ISBN 9781368024051 (board) •
ISBN 9781368056205 (ebook) Subjects: CYAC: Mythology, Roman—Fiction. •
Camps—Fiction. • Diaries—Fiction. Classification: LCC PZ7.R4829 Cao 2020
• DDC [Fic]—dc23 LC record available at https://lccn.loc.gov/2019041794

Visit www.DisneyBooks.com
Follow @ReadRiordan

SUSTAINABLE FORESTRY INITIATIVE   Certified Sourcing
www.sfiprogram.org
SFI-00993
Logo Applies to Text Stock Only

To all campers, past and present

CONTENTS

From Reyna Avila Ramírez-Arellano,
Praetor of the Twelfth Legion Fulminata:

This journal has been reprinted with the author's permission at my request. It is my hope, and that of my fellow praetor, Frank Zhang, that this record of one *probatio*'s experiences will serve a dual purpose: first, as an introduction to Camp Jupiter for all new recruits and, second, as a valuable reminder that there are outside forces who seek to destroy our way of life. Let Claudia's story be a warning that we must be ever vigilant if we are to survive.

We can never know where or when the next attack is coming . . . only that it is inevitable.

SPQR forever!
—RARA

DAY I: *I Made It!*

Oh, my gods, it's my first night in the Fourth Cohort barracks! I scored a great bunk right next to the window, and I'm writing by the light of an ancient Roman oil lamp. Sooo cool! I want to record everything I'm feeling, everything I've seen and been through to get here. But it's lamps-out now. So, until next time . . .

One hour later . . .

First item on tomorrow's to-do list: Find a store that sells earplugs. The girl in the bunk next to me snores loud enough to rattle the tiles out of a mosaic. Explains why my bed was up for grabs when I first arrived.

I'm holed up in the girls' latrine now, writing because sleeping is a lost cause. As far as bathrooms go, this one's pretty awesome. Marble tile everywhere with gold-plated touches, like the hinges on the stall doors. Seeing those hinges makes me a little homesick, actually. Dad would geek out over them. I don't get why he loves restoring old hardware so much, but hey, he earns a living doing it, so no judgment.

Apparently, making money is something that comes naturally to a legacy of Mercury. "A legacy of Mercury." Yikes. It's still sinking in that Dad and I are descended from a Roman god, and one of the twelve biggies of Olympus, no less. Especially because I knew next to nothing about my family until two months ago. I still don't know anything about my mom except her name, Cardi, and what she looks like. *Looked* like. I found a picture of her stashed away in Dad's room. In the photo she was maybe in her early twenties, and we have the same wavy dark hair, dark eyes, high cheekbones, and large nose. She was leaning against the frame of an open doorway, one hand resting on her stomach. I think she was pregnant then . . . with me.

Right. Moving on.

I had no clue about the Mercury connection until my twelfth birthday, when Dad gave me an old scroll that showed his family's genealogy. Three generations back, there's Great-Granddad, the messenger of the gods, also the god of merchants and shopkeepers, thieves and tricksters, and travelers. Wears a lot of hats, he does, all of them winged.

Full disclosure, Dad: I thought you'd gone bonkers when you showed me that scroll. And when you told me about your past and my future— that like you, one day soon I'd be summoned by the wolf goddess, Lupa, and brought to a crumbling old mansion in Sonoma, California, where her immortal wolf pack would train me to be a Roman soldier. (I have this to say about that: Worst. Campout. Ever.) Assuming I passed all their tests—aka, didn't die a horrible, wolf-inflicted death—I'd then trek southward through a monster-infested wilderness (second-worst campout ever) to Camp Jupiter, where I'd present your letter of recommendation to whoever was in charge and hope I'd be accepted into the ranks of the Twelfth Legion Fulminata.

Which brings me to this question: How much would it suck to go through all that and *not* get into a cohort? Answer: A lot.

Not that new recruits need to worry about rejection these days. According to my centurion, Leila, the legion's numbers were badly depleted last summer. Something about a war involving the primordial earth goddess Gaea, a bunch of giants, a humungous statue of the Greek goddess Athena, and a Greek demigod camp. Good news: Camp Jupiter helped save the world! ☺ Bad news: Camp Jupiter lost a lot of people while helping save the world. ☹ More bad news: Something funky happened to demigod communications soon after our victory. Which Leila says likely spells more trouble coming our way. . . .

Anyway, Dad, sorry I doubted you, because it all went down just like you said it would. And now I'm here, with my official probatio name tag around my neck: CLAUDIA, FOURTH COHORT. So thank you for the heads-up. And for this journal. If I ever have kids, they can read about my life here so they're ready when their turns come.

Welp, time to head back to bed. Tomorrow I'll get my first real look at Camp Jupiter. And the first place I'll visit?

Wherever they sell earplugs.

DAY II: *Um, What?*

Things I learned today:

1) Oatmeal is not the preferred breakfast food among campers. At least, that's the impression I got from the disgusted looks when the *aurae* delivered my bowl of it this morning. Well, to each their own, I say.

2) Bargain shopping on the Via Praetoria is easy when you're descended from the god of shopkeepers. I was on the lookout for earplugs when I spotted a toy store that sells Roman-deity action figures. Mercury was front and center in the window, wearing nothing but a short toga. Now, I'm sure that look was all the rage in ancient times,

and the figure was pretty buff, but still, I was a little embarrassed to see mini Great-Granddad standing there like that. Plus, something about his eyes reminded me of Dad. . . . Anyway, I bought the doll. And I think Great-Granddad approved and loaned me his powers, because somehow I convinced the shop owner to throw in Mercury's accessories— winged cap, winged sandals, caduceus, and tiny sack of coins—for free. Short toga included (thank gods).

3) Weird things happen on Temple Hill.

I learned this last lesson while checking out Mercury's temple after my delicious and nutritious breakfast. Compared to the dinky shrines of the minor gods and goddesses, Great-Granddad's place isn't too shabby. A rectangular structure with marble columns all around the outside, an ornate fresco above the entrance, and inside, a life-size statue of the god himself.

The weird thing happened when I approached the altar. Someone had put two message bins there in honor of Mercury's role as messenger to the gods. The bin marked OUTGOING was overflowing with notes, but the INCOMING one was empty, a sad reminder that our communications have flatlined.

Still, I added a note of my own to the outbox. Just a little *Hey, Great-Granddad, what's the word from Olympus?* I was about to leave when I heard a fluttering sound. A piece of paper had appeared in the INCOMING bin. Written on it was the Roman numeral twelve—XII—and nothing else.

Now, it's possible that the note fell out of the OUTGOING bin. But it's equally possible that Mercury sent it. Either way, it felt important, and I didn't want anyone else to find it. So I stuffed the note in my pocket and didn't give it another thought for the rest of the day.

Yeah, right. That paper has been torturing me for hours! Where did it come from? What does *XII* mean? Twelve Olympians? Twelve months in a year? Twelve eggs in a dozen? My age? Argh!

It doesn't matter that my roommate is snoring again and I forgot to buy earplugs. Thanks to XII, I'm not getting any sleep tonight anyway.

DAY III: *Ow!*

I once saw a T-shirt that read EVERYTHING HURTS AND I'M DYING. I need one of those. That way, when someone asks how my first weapons practice went, I can just point to my chest. Because *ow*.

Yes, sports fans, in just one session in the Colosseum, I managed to slice my hand with a *gladius* and stab my thigh with a *pugio*. I twanged my cheek with a bowstring and pierced my foot with an arrow. (Note to self: Never wear sandals to weapons practice again.) I launched a weird weighted-dart thingy called a *plumbata* into the stands. And for my grand finale, I clocked my instructor in the head with the butt of my *pilum* when I reared back to throw. (She turned it into a teachable moment about why we each wear a *galea*, immediately

Sling it with the rope???

followed by a second teachable moment in which she explained galea means *helmet*.)

Later, she asked me—nicely—how I ever managed to survive Lupa's training. I told her the truth: booby traps. I admitted that tricks like covering a pit with branches or dropping a net from

the treetops on an unsuspecting enemy weren't very Roman, but they'd kept mc alive. To my surprise, she pointed out that they dug trenches for the camp's war games

At least I had this...

15

all the time, and that a weighted net, along with a trident and dagger, were the weapons favored by the *retiarius*, a type of gladiator. She promised to introduce me to the current retiarius champion after the next gladiator games. If we hit it off, he might even let me test-drive his weapons.

So maybe I'm not a lost cause after all.

On a less positive note, I still have no clue as to what XII means. I'll visit Mercury's temple again before classes start tomorrow. Maybe a new message has appeared.

DAY IV: *Nice God-Crypt, Mars*

If Mercury sent any other messages, someone else got to them first. Still, the morning wasn't a total waste. I had some time to kill before my first lecture—"Great Roman Inventions: Concrete," which was actually more interesting than it sounds (not) and taught by Vitellius, a purple-hued *Lar* with a captivating speaking voice (double not)— so I toured a few other temples. I loved Bellona's fierce-warrior vibe and Jupiter's blinged-out sanctuary. Pluto's zombie-apocalypse theme? Not so much.

But the one that really spoke to me was the

Temple of Mars Ultor. I mean, who wouldn't dig that red marble crypt with its cast-iron doors? And inside, that massive statue of the Avenger (no, not one of *those* Avengers), his scarred face scowling

and his spear raised as if to strike whoever dares to enter. Let's not forget the display wall of human skulls and assorted weapons, from the kind that slice and dice to the kind that leave bullet-

shaped holes. Even the ceiling pays tribute, with eleven identical and bizarre-looking shields that form the letter *M*.

That military man-cave—sorry, god-crypt— was built to intimidate, but the decor was so over-the-top, I broke into giggles while looking at it. I got out of there before I lost control, though. I'm not stupid enough to risk insulting the war god.

But I'm pretty sure I insulted his son. When I came out of Mars's temple, I ran right into Praetor Frank Zhang. It was like hitting a brick wall, the guy is so solid. That should have sobered me up, but I took one look at him and started laughing all over again. I couldn't even explain what was so funny. What would I have said? *Your face reminds me of how ridiculous your dad's temple is*?

I feel bad about it, though. I would have apologized at dinner, but Praetor Frank wasn't there.

Time to go—gotta review the recipe for Roman concrete in case there's a quiz tomorrow.

DAY V: *A Sack Full of Dead Rats*

It was touch-and-go there for a moment when the centurions spun the chore wheel this afternoon. After the full-fledged legionnaires got the fun jobs—testing the catapults, taking Hannibal the elephant for a lumber, clapping chalk dust out of the erasers—I was sure it would land on SEWER UNCLOGGING when it was my turn.

Instead, I hit the jackpot with AQUEDUCT CLEAN-OUT. Or so I thought. Turns out aqueduct clean-out does not mean plucking a leaf or two from the structure that ferries clean water into camp. No, it means slogging, sometimes crawling, through a maze of underground tunnels filled with ice-cold water and removing anything that isn't ice-cold water. This includes dead rats, hair of both human and unknown origin, plastic trash bags (Come on, people! Reduce, reuse, recycle, remember?), and other disgusting flotsam and jetsam that could contaminate our bathing and drinking supply.

My partner in slime was a demigod son of Vulcan named Blaise. Yes, the god of forges and fire has a son named Blaise. But I didn't laugh. After all, I'm named for Emperor Claudius, who everyone believed was a fool because he stuttered and had a limp. He ended up being a decent ruler—even conquered Britain, the only emperor to do so—but still. I'm not going to get all judgy about someone else's name when mine conjures up a word like *clod*.

I figured Blaise and I would hang out together, chitchat about life as a probatio, maybe sing a few rousing clean-out songs to get us in the mood. But he just grabbed his sack and his trash picker and sloshed off. I showed him, though. I trucked right after him down that tunnel . . . and instantly got lost. Ha-ha! Being descended from the god of travelers doesn't do anything for you in underground waterways, apparently.

I wandered around for an hour, shoving rat

carcasses into my sack and praying my headlamp didn't go out, before I finally spotted a ladder illuminated by daylight. When I reached it, I saw that it led up to a circular opening blocked by iron bars. I figured it was either a dead end or an exit, and I was definitely ready to exit. I climbed to the top as best I could with my hands full, and the grate opened easily when I pushed it. I swung my rat bag and picker up onto the ledge and then lifted myself out of the hole . . .

Right into a big fat load of trouble that began with two metal dogs and ended with Praetor Reyna.

How was I supposed to know that ladder was a secret back entrance into the *principia*? That's what I would have said if I could have. But I was too busy screaming in terror as the silver and gold dogs flew at me. Luckily, Praetor Reyna called them off before they could rip open my throat, which allowed me the opportunity to explain that I was lost. I showed her my sack full of dead rodents as proof of my chore duty. Then I demonstrated that the grate she insisted was magically locked was, in fact, not. She had a frowny face while I was talking, but she sent me on my way with zero metal-dog bites, so I guess she believed me.

Either that, or she wanted the dead rats out of her office. Don't know, don't care, just happy to be alive!

DAY VI: *Bruises and Baked Goods*

I made a friend in the Fourth today! Her name is Janice, and she's the daughter of—wait for it—Janus, the two-faced god of choices, doorways, and beginnings and endings. (Blaise, Janice . . . What *is* it with godly parents and their demigod kids' names? Who's next? A kid named Roman?) Janice is in her second month on probatio, but she knows a ton about Camp Jupiter because she was born and raised in New Rome. How cool is *that*?

Man, I would have loved to have grown up there. Marble, gold, and red-tile roof buildings, ginormous fountains and gardens, cobblestone streets with shops that sell togas and chariots—it's like time-warping back to ancient Rome. Janice says gods and goddesses sometimes sneak down from Olympus to hang out there. Some even disguise themselves as humans and start families with retired legionnaires! I don't know if that's true, but if it is . . . mind = blown.

In fact, the only negative about New Rome might be the panhandling fauns, and they're mostly harmless hippies who like lazing in the sun, scratching themselves, and snacking on trash. (I'd judge, but I eat junk food, so . . .) I got a little sad when I saw one young faun named Elon nibbling on soda-can tabs strung on a string. Not because I felt bad for him. (Well, maybe a little—the kid was sitting all alone next to a trash can.) But mostly because the tabs reminded me of the candy necklaces Dad used to buy me when I was little.

Back to Janice. We met on the Field of Mars—the pockmarked, boulder-and-rubble-strewn meadow where weekly war games among cohorts take place—during Fort-Building 101. (Today's assignment: Build a fort. Tomorrow's assignment: Build a fort. Day after tomorrow's assignment: Build a fort.) My job was to construct an arched doorway. Since I aced wooden-gate installation in the previous class—picked up a little hinge knowledge from watching Dad, apparently—I figured an arch would be no sweat. But the stupid stone blocks

wouldn't stay in place. When they fell on me a third time, I blurted some inappropriate words.

That's when this girl with wide-set eyes and long braids—Janice—yelled over, "Hey! Stick a keystone in it, will ya?" I thought she was warning me to watch my language. Turns out she meant it literally—that I should fit a wedge-shaped block in the top center spot. I did, and presto! The keystone locked the other blocks in place. Instant arch!

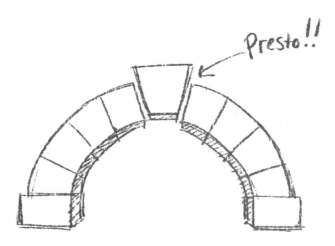

Presto!!

After class, I bought Janice a pastry from Bombilo's café to thank her for saving me from further bodily harm. It took her forever to decide on the one to get, which I thought was hilarious since she's the daughter of the god of choices. She could have taken all day as far as I was concerned, because Bombilo's smelled sooo good. Just thinking about that cinnamon and sugar and vanilla and coffee odor now is making my mouth water! My merchant/shopkeeper genes are tingling too. I know I could rake in serious dough (ha!) if I could bottle up and sell that scent. Multipurpose spritz bottles . . . Yes, I can smell the profits already! (Double ha!)

Janice and I bonded over our sugar-crusted pastries while relaxing in hammocks on the Fourth barracks front porch. We talked about everything from growing up as the only children of single parents (not an issue for either of us) to our near-death experiences with Lupa (very much an issue for both of us) to tomorrow's *testudo*—turtle, tortoise, whatever; I'm trying to use the Latin terms when I can—practice (only an issue if we're shoulder to shoulder beneath that shell of shields with a garlic-scented mouth-breather). We're in the same ID the Deity class, so later tonight we're going to quiz each other on the names and attributes of minor gods and goddesses.

And now I'm going to admit something I've avoided thinking about: Even though I'm surrounded by people wherever I go, I've been lonely here. But thanks to Janice, that's over now. ☺

DAY VII: *The Girl of My Dreams*

Can't say I hadn't been warned.

My first morning in the Fourth, Leila had called me to her bunk for a *here's what's what* talk. She explained the different ranks within the legion (probatio, legionnaire, centurion, praetor) and told me I could leapfrog right to legionnaire if I did some mega-heroic unselfish deed. No pressure, she said, though it would boost the Fourth's cred if I did. Then she went over Camp Jupiter's ground rules, stuff like no taking a giant eagle out for a joy ride, no plotting to overthrow your praetor, no short-sheeting the senators' togas no matter how hilarious a prank that might be. Punishments for rule-breaking range from extra chores to banishment to being sewn into a bag with angry weasels. (That last one got a solid *yikes* from me.)

Finally, she warned me that probatios often have wild and crazy dreams after arriving at camp. Being plopped into the middle of ancient Rome's last remaining outpost and surrounded by godly influences—and maybe even the occasional god, if Janice was right about them visiting New Rome—triggers the visions, they think. Sometimes the dreams are harmless, but other times they're horrible nightmares that warn of impending danger. So if I ever wake up screaming, Leila said, I should come find her. Because the screams alone wouldn't be enough to alert her that something was wrong, apparently.

My first nights here were mercifully nightmare-free. Tonight, though . . . well, I didn't wake up screaming, but my dream did have some uber-disturbing moments. Here's what I remember:

A frizzy-haired girl about my age approached the Decumanian Gate, the camp's western entrance. Her ratty sneakers flapped with every step. Her threadbare dress hung like a filthy rag on her skinny four-foot-nothing frame. She looked like a stiff breeze could knock her over, and yet something about her—her clenched teeth, the tightness around her dark, heavily lashed eyes, the fleet of flies buzzing around her head—made my dream-self uneasy.

When she reached the gate, Terminus, the god who guards our borders, popped up. (I find Terminus fascinating. I mean, the guy is just a marble head and torso, no arms, no legs—and yet I swear he has a stick up his butt.) He demanded to

33

see her identification. But when she thrust her letter of recommendation at him, he drew back, shook his head violently, and refused to let her enter.

A centurion of the Fourth Cohort arrived then. He wore the usual Roman gear—helmet, chain mail, leather arm and leg greaves, dagger, combat boots with piked cleats, sword, and . . . Gods, I'm exhausted just writing it all down—forget wearing it! I took the guy for a modern-day sentry until I saw his ripped jeans and the flannel shirt tied around his waist. Those fashion choices hinted at 1990s grunge rock. But it wasn't until he removed his helmet that I knew I was glimpsing a scene from the past.

Because the centurion was my dad.

Not the guy I know and love, with his pudgy dad bod, dark brown hair, and nondescript clothes, but back when he was a high-ranking, scraggy

teenage member of the Twelfth Legion Fulminata. With a cringe-y bleached-blond cowlick, no less.

He stepped forward and overruled Terminus. The god threw his nonexistent arms up in disgust while Dad beckoned to the girl with a welcoming smile. That smile changed to alarm mixed with mild revulsion—the same expression he got the time he found a week-old pizza box festering under my bed—when the girl shoved her papers into his hand and pushed past him into camp. Eyes wide, Dad glanced at Terminus, who shot him a superior *told you so* look before vanishing.

The scene dissolved. New ones tumbled rapid-fire through my mind: The assembled legion stumbling back to let the girl pass. The aurae flinging food at her from far across the mess hall. Her bunkmates whispering about her behind their hands. Hannibal the elephant letting out an alarmed trumpet when she neared.

The dream shifted again. Now Dad stood at attention before his praetors inside the principia. The praetors questioned him about the new girl. He shook his head and said he'd tried, he really had, but no one in the cohort could stand to be around her. Her presence was disrupting the Fourth's ability to work as a unit. Something needed to be done. The praetors looked grave but nodded.

The dream spun back to the barracks. It was after midnight, but the girl was out of bed. She had a tattered knapsack over one shoulder, and I knew instinctively she was running away. Before she sneaked outside, though, she tipped over a garbage can and kicked the rotting contents all over the barracks floor.

Then she scowled. Not at her bunkmates—at me. At least that's what it seemed like.

That's when I woke up. As soon as my heart stopped racing, I grabbed this journal and came here to my favorite latrine to ponder the dream's significance. It was weird seeing Dad at that age, and I was no fan of the girl's scowl, but overall, the dream didn't seem to foretell any danger. I mean, everything in it had happened years ago. So no reason to rouse Leila.

Especially if . . . Well, what if the dream was a different kind of warning—a warning that not every demigod or legacy finds a place at Camp Jupiter? I'm afraid that if I go to Leila, she might think I had the dream because I don't really belong here.

So yeah. I'm going to keep the dream to myself. After all, the fewer people who know about my dad's cowlick, the better. . . .

DAY VIII: *A Thrilla on Aquila*

Today was super fun, except for the near-death experience.

It happened midway through the course Intro to Elephants, Unicorns, and Giant Eagles, which I'd signed up for because, well, elephants, unicorns, and giant eagles. (A totally misleading description, BTW, as there is only one elephant here. Unless they're hiding a spare pachyderm somewhere. Possible, though not likely. I think.) The class met at the stables, which are located uncomfortably close to the Fifth Cohort barracks. How those guys stand the stench is beyond me. (Note to self: The

Fifth would be the perfect market for my spritz bottles of Bombilo's Café Scent!)

Eye-watering stink aside, the class was cool. I learned the proper technique for making medicinal unicorn-horn shavings (cheese grater applied gently to horn). I scrubbed Hannibal behind the ears with a sudsy push broom (if elephants could purr, his motor would have been rumbling overtime). I fed dead rats—probably the ones I'd collected earlier in the week—to hungry giant eagles.

And I stepped in a catastrophic amount of poop. The Elephants, Unicorns, and Giant Eagles class should come with a *no sandals* warning. After my third encounter, I asked the instructors a two-part question: Whose job is it to clean up all this poop, and where does the poop go?

Answer: Here's a shovel and a compostable garbage bag. Use one to fill the other. Tie the bag up tight. And then get out of the way, pronto.

Well, my pronto wasn't pronto enough. Which is why I suddenly went airborne when a giant

female eagle named Aquila (Latin for *eagle*; wonder which clever legionnaire named her?) swooped in and snatched my poop bag in her talons.

Full disclosure: I clung to that smelly sack as if my life depended on it. Actually, I'm pretty sure it did, because oh my *gods* we flew high. Camp Jupiter disappeared in the distance. Or where I guessed the camp was, because the Mist, that magical force that shields our world from mortals, had disguised it as open hills and forests. I'm still learning to look through the Mist, but when I squinted, I could just make out the Little Tiber ribboning through the meadow and the lake at the foot of Temple Hill.

We flew on, Aquila, the poop bag, and me, until a rolling expanse of rotting garbage—the local landfill—came into view. The eagle dove to deposit her load. The descent was like the worst kind of roller coaster ride—full speed straight down, no twists or turns—and the garbage odor was even worse than the stables. (Ooh! Another outlet for Bombilo's Café Scent!) I scrambled up on Aquila's back to get my nose above the stink.

Not a second too soon, either. A worker in a hard hat and a bright yellow safety vest emerged from her trailer. I flattened myself into the eagle's neck feathers just in case the Mist wasn't working. I risked a peek when we took off, though.

The worker had taken off her sunglasses. I couldn't see her eyes under her hard hat, but I could tell she was watching us. And she was smiling. Not a nice *thanks for the giant bag of poop, come again soon* smile—a nasty, knowing smile that gave me the shivers. I couldn't get away from her and that landfill fast enough.

Not that I was eager to get back to camp,

because I figured I'd be in trouble. But my instructors were too relieved to see me in one piece to yell at me. Well, not too loudly or for too long, anyway.

Here's the thing, though: I'd do it again. Not the poop-bag flight or the landfill part, but the return journey. Because open-air soaring via giant-eagle express was *a-maz-ing*. And maybe I'm crazy, but I think Aquila liked having me along for the ride.

That's how I interpreted the little beak nudge she gave me when I slipped off, anyway. Sure, I'd get stuck with extra chores if I took her for an unauthorized flight, but honestly? It'd be worth it!

DAY IX: *So Not Cool*

Someone has been messing with my stuff! Specifically, with my Mercury action figure. Before Janice and I left to visit Temple Hill, I posed him like the statue in Great-Granddad's sanctuary—leaning casually against a post, ankles crossed, his sack of coins in one hand and his caduceus in the crook of his other elbow.

But now his legs are bent as if he's about to spring into action. One arm is raised overhead, his caduceus held like a spear. Posed like that, he doesn't look like Mercury anymore. He looks like a warrior. Almost like Mars, minus the threatening snarl. And his coin purse is missing.

I'm sure someone's just playing a prank on me, but still . . . I'm going to ask Janice if I should say something to our centurions.

Later . . .

I took Janice's advice and didn't bother Leila. I'm glad I didn't, because I just found the coin purse tucked under my pillow. Inside was a slip of parchment with two words, *Invenient MV*, inside an oval with a squiggly bottom. No clue what that oval signifies, but I've got chills. Because the handwriting is the same as in my *XII* note.

I know *invenient* is Latin for *find,* and it's used when the thing to be found is male. Which means *MV* is a boy or a man. But who is he? I don't know anyone here with those initials. Why am I supposed to look for him, and what am I supposed to do if and when I find him? And what, if anything, does the message have to do with *XII* or my Mercury figure being posed to look like Mars? Argh!!!

Well, I guess the only one who can answer those questions is the mysterious MV. So tomorrow, I'll start looking for him. It shouldn't take long. After all, there are only two hundred of us in the legion, and not all of us are male.

Of course, if MV isn't a member of the Twelfth . . . it could be a while before I invenient him.

DAY X: *Claudia the Clumsy*

Welp, today has been totally awesome, she wrote sarcastically.

I spent the morning asking if anyone knew who MV was. No luck, and when I started getting funny looks, I decided to back-burner the investigation for the time being. Then this afternoon I was trapped digging a trench with a chatterbox who spoke in question marks: "My name is, like, Lynda? I'm in the Second Cohort? My favorite store is the Sandal Shoppe?" The only time she shut up was when I accidentally-on-purpose tossed a shovelful of dirt in her face.

49

And then there was tonight, when I played in my first deathball match. (Deathball™! Like paintball, only with poison and acid and fireballs launched from a mini *manubalista*! Painful for all ages!) It should have been exciting, especially since Janice and I came up with a totally boss strategy we called the Janus. Basically, we fired our projectiles while crouched back to back behind our *scutum* (which I kept calling *sputum* until Janice explained that one was a large curved shield and the other was the wet mucusy stuff we cough up when we're sick; I probably won't confuse the two again). We looked like a two-headed, four-footed garbage bin shuffling around the field. But we withstood all attacks!

Or we did until I slipped on a loose deathball and fell in the trench I'd dug with Question Mark Lynda. Janice escaped unscathed, but it was pretty much open season on me. My bruises will heal, but my scutum is dinged up worse than the hood of a car caught in a hailstorm. I'll have to take it to the forges to get the dents banged out.

The icing on the cake? I twisted my ankle. So, if the ambrosia and nectar don't heal it, people will now have a legit reason to call me Claudia the Clumsy.

DAY XI: *Mess in the Mess*

Things were ugly in the mess hall this morning, and not just because an unprecedented number of legionnaires stumbled in with serious bed head. No, the trouble was because the food service was on the fritz. Instead of pancakes, bacon, and fruit, the wind spirits delivered nothing but hot, steamy oatmeal. Not a problem for me, but for the others . . . yikes.

Hangry legionnaires were gearing up to storm the kitchens when a big black raven—aka Praetor Frank—flew in and announced that donuts from Bombilo's were on the way.

Much as I like oatmeal, I wasn't going to pass up free donuts. So I headed outside to scrape my half-eaten bowl into a waste bin.

That's when I spotted Elon standing on his

tippy-hooves and peeking in through a window. Fauns aren't allowed inside the mess hall, but they occasionally sneak in for a quick mouthful of tasty cutlery. Elon is a lot younger than the other fauns, though—his horns are barely noticeable and the fur on his legs still looks baby-fine—so I figured he was too intimidated to break the rules. I knew the legionnaires would protest even more loudly if I gave him a precious donut, so I went over and offered him my oatmeal instead.

Mistake. First off, the dude reeked like he'd been rolling in wet, slimy dumpster juice. Then he looked at my oatmeal as if it were *purgamentorum derelinquere caeno*. (That's Latin for *sewage sludge*. I plan to hurl it at my enemy during the next war games. The phrase, not the actual sludge. Although . . . hmm.) And in case his disgusted expression didn't get the message across, he gave me a verbal slap, too: "Elon doesn't need your leftovers. Elon gets the pick of the litter."

I'm sorry, but anyone who refers to himself in the third person and brags about getting the choicest trash does not deserve my oatmeal, thank you very much. So I emptied my bowl and went back inside to the sad discovery that the last available donut was covered in coconut. Talk about purgamentorum derelinquere caeno.

As bad as my morning was, it was nothing compared to what the aurae were going through. Usually, they're invisible. But today they were so agitated they flickered like faulty lightbulbs. That's how I realized that the food service mix-up wasn't their doing. Which leads to these million-denarius questions: What went wrong? What will we eat if the mess hall is still messed up at lunch? And finally: Why would you ruin a perfectly good donut with *coconut*?

DAY XII: *Two Words: Air Freshener*

There comes a moment in every young probatio's life when she realizes she should have peed before putting on her armor. For me, that moment came when I reached the top of the watchtower for my first shift on sentry duty. I tried to pay attention while my partner, Julius, a seasoned legionnaire with three tattooed lines above his dad Mars's symbol, explained how to fire a mounted crossbow. But I was so seriously hydrated I had to cut him off and request permission to use the facilities.

He was very understanding (not). I believe his exact words were, "Stop dancing from foot to foot and just *go* already!" I'm pretty sure I set the camp record for racing down a flight of stairs while shedding armor.

The nearest facility was a unisex single-seater that looked like a Porta-Poo portable toilet dressed up in marble tiles. To my horror, the little sign by the door handle read OCCUPIED. A female voice inside confirmed that fact. "Mission accomplished!" she crowed.

Yeah, that was a weird thing to say in a bathroom, but I didn't care, because it meant she was done and I'd reached the desperation point. And yet she still didn't come out! So after waiting a hot second, I pounded on the door and asked if she could *please* hurry up.

I heard some shuffling, then the toilet flushed, the sign shifted to VACANT, and the occupant emerged. Not a girl. Not a boy, either, but

Elon. I'm sure I looked surprised because, well, I'd assumed fauns used the great outdoors as their toilet. But judging from the stench that trailed out after him . . . um, no.

I'd also assumed all fauns were like Don, the faun who once tried to sweet-talk me out of denarii so he could buy donuts. But Elon said just two words: "All yours." His high, reedy voice didn't sound anything like the one I'd heard. That led me to a third assumption: He hadn't been alone in the bathroom.

But I was wrong a third time, because no one else came out, and when I stepped inside, the bathroom was empty. Well, except for some flies, and they didn't say anything except *bzzz-bzzz-bzzz* while I did my biz.

My sentry partner just smirked when I told him about the mysterious female voice. Said Elon was probably meeting up with a water naiad who flushed herself away when I knocked. I wondered aloud where she ended up. And then I stopped wondering because I remembered the smell and . . . gross.

Thing is, I'm not sure my partner was right. Because the voice didn't sound girlish or flirty. It sounded raspy and triumphant. And Elon looked relieved, though not the way I did after I'd used the facilities. So now I'm wondering . . . what was *that* all about?

DAY XIII: *Bang On!*

Breakthrough! I found out who MV is. Or was. Or is it *is*? What's the proper way to refer to a ghost, anyway?

The source of my info was none other than Blaise, my rat-sacking aqueduct-clean-out partner. He was on duty at the forges when I brought my scutum in for ding repair. Stepping into that workspace was like crawling inside an asthmatic dragon, all hot and humid with weird wheezing sounds. The only light source was the orange glow of the furnace until Blaise flicked a switch and a bank of harsh fluorescent overheads came on. Kind of fizzled the volcanic atmosphere, if I'm honest.

I didn't think Blaise knew who I was—I mean, we're not in the same cohort and we'd literally spent thirty seconds together on chore duty last week—so I was shocked when he greeted me by name. Of course, he could have just read it off my probatio tag, but still . . . A for effort. He laid my shield on the worktable and ran his fingers over it, his brow furrowed. When I asked if he could fix it, he made a face. "Uh, *duh*. It's what I do." Then he picked up a little hammer and started banging away at the dents.

I wasn't sure if I was supposed to stick around until he finished, but I did because Blaise was such stimulating company. Ha! Wrong. I stuck around because I'd spotted the net of a retiarius gladiator in need of a few replacement weights. Since it was already broken, I didn't see any harm in taking it for a spin.

The problem with whirling a poorly weighted net inside a crowded space is that things get knocked over. And tangled up. And ever-so-slightly damaged. Whoops.

One of the things I knocked over was an old leather-bound book filled with beautiful sketches of weapons and shields and armor. Blaise yelped when he saw me paging through it. Turns out the book is one of a kind and contains the life's work of an ancient master craftsman and demigod son of Vulcan, Mamurius Veturius.

MV.

I wasn't sure the craftsman was *my* MV until Blaise mentioned that Mamurius is a ghost who usually hangs around the forges. That's when I realized the squiggly oval around the initials on my note looked a lot like the outline of a ghost. So if I'm right—and I sure hope I am, because this is the only lead I've got—then I finally have MV's identity.

What I don't have is his actual incorporeal presence. Blaise hasn't seen Mamurius at the forges for over a week. Which he says is weird, because the ghost is *always* lurking around there.

So, MV is not only a dead guy, but a dead end unless I can track him down. And how the heck am I supposed to do that? The guy can appear and disappear at will. He could be anywhere!

Blaise might be able to tell me about him, I suppose. He and Mamurius are both Vulcan's sons, after all, which makes them half brothers. (Yikes. My head hurts just thinking about that.) But after the mess my net-twirling caused in the forges, I'm not sure I'm his favorite probatio right now. In fact, I think he was adding dents to my scutum when I left.

So for now, I'll forge on alone. (Ha!)

DAY XIV: *Oh, Rats!*

When I heard the ear-piercing scream tonight, I figured someone in the Fourth was having a nightmare of the impending-danger variety. Then I realized the shrieks weren't coming from the barracks but from inside the bathhouse.

For our safety, nobody is supposed to be in the baths after eleven, because there are no lifeguards on duty. Janice says the real reason the doors are locked is to thwart romantically inclined legionnaires from getting up to shenanigans in there. That thwarting can be thwarted, though, if you know about the secret entrance to the main pool. Which everybody does, although not many people use it, because you have to swim underwater through a narrow concrete pipe, then squeeze through a small mesh gate that leads into the pool. You'd better hope you're an underwater-breathing descendent of Neptune if you get stuck in there.

Apparently, a girl and a boy from the First Cohort thought the risk was worth it, because they sneaked in via the not-so-secret entrance tonight. I'm thinking their lovey-dovey mood evaporated when they surfaced, though.

Because dead rats.

Hundreds of them. Floating in the pool. Blocking the hot-springs water supply. Clogging the drains. Even hanging from the basket for used towels. I can't imagine anything more totally, completely, scream-inducingly disgusting.

And mysterious, too, because no one can

explain how so many rats got in there so quickly. The filtration system is shut off when the baths close, so they weren't pumped in with the water. And the lifeguard swears the place was clean when he locked up at eleven. The couple sneaked in around eleven fifteen. Could someone have broken in and distributed all those rats in just fifteen minutes? Didn't seem likely.

We were all scratching our heads when it came out that the lifeguard, a member of the Third, had

a crush on the girl. The couple accused him of planting the rats to disrupt their date. The lifeguard denied it. The First rallied behind the young lovers and started blaming the lifeguard. The Third jumped in and flung those accusations right back at the couple, and then at the whole First Cohort. The First retaliated with venom. (The verbal kind, not actual venom. At least . . . I don't *think* so.)

Things were escalating out of control when Frank and Reyna showed up. They listened to

both sides, deliberated for a few minutes, and then ordered the First and the Third to clean up the mess together.

I like thinking about legionnaires from the First picking up dead rats, because so many of them are . . . hmm, what's the best way to describe members of that cohort? Oh yes. Obnoxious jerks who think they're all that and a bag of chips.

I feel bad for the lifeguard, though. The only thing he's guilty of is liking someone who didn't like him back. Hope that never happens to me.

DAY XV:
Good Old-Fashioned Book Learning

It was a beautiful sunshine-filled morning, right up until it started raining poop. Not on me, thank gods, because *ick*.

I feel for the Second, though. They were on shovel-and-bag duty at the stables. But the compostable sacks must have been defective. Every time the giant eagles went airborne with their loads, the plastic ripped open and . . . well, it wasn't a good time for those caught underneath, that's for sure. Or for anybody caught next to them afterward. Not even a spritz of Bombilo's Café Scent could have cut through that stink.

On a more positive note, the praetors have canceled this afternoon's marching practice while they look into the faulty-bag issue. Which frees up my schedule to invenient MV!

Later . . .

No luck locating MV yet. But thanks to a visit to New Rome University's library during my free time this afternoon, I know a ton more about Mamurius Veturius.

The library rivals some of the temples for architectural fabulousness. Sunlight streams into the main reading room through the oculus, the round skylight in the center of the gilded dome ceiling. Colorful tile mosaics of deities, famous Romans, and mythical creatures decorate the walls. One candlelit hallway is paved with stones engraved with the names of lost heroes. Some of those stones look worn and ancient, but others are brand-new. Heroes who died in last summer's conflicts, I think.

Here's hoping no new stones are added for a long, long time.

The library's shelves are chock-full of scrolls and books. I'd probably still be searching the biography section except the exact volume I needed, *Who Made What When and For Whom and Why: Ancient Roman Craftsmen*, literally fell into my hands. I swear I saw a dark-haired woman peeking at me through the empty space where the slim book had been. But when I blinked and looked again, she was gone.

I took the book to a cozy window seat and flipped through the pages, looking for an entry for Mamurius Veturius. It was so brief, I almost missed it. Here's what I found out:

Mamurius Veturius was master craftsman to King Numa, the ruler who took over the throne after Romulus, Rome's founder, died. Numa was one of the good guys, famous for building temples (including one honoring Janus, Janice's dad), writing books of laws, and keeping peace in the kingdom for forty-three years. (Not too shabby!) The gods apparently approved of Numa, because at some point during his reign, they sent him an ornate cello-shaped shield called an *ancile*, along with this promise: So long as this ancile is safe, Rome will endure.

Meaning, I guess, that if the ancile goes missing, Rome will go kaboom.

That's where Mamurius Veturius came in. King Numa instructed his craftsman to make eleven identical copies of the ancile. That way, if someone tried to steal the ancile in order to destroy

Rome, he'd have no clue which was the real one. The duplicates were so good that only Mamurius himself knew which one the original was. But just to be extra safe, King Numa stashed the twelve ancilia in a temple only a crazy person would dare to defile: the Temple of Mars Ultor.

I've been in Mars's temple—or the modern-day replica, anyway. I saw a bunch of one-of-a-kind weapons in there . . . and an M made of eleven identical cello-shaped shields.

Eleven. Not twelve. Not . . . *XII.*

I'm thinking those eleven are Mamurius's duplicates and that the original is hidden somewhere else in camp. Because it must be here. Otherwise Camp Jupiter, the living, breathing testament to Rome's endurance, wouldn't exist. Right?

I searched other books for info about Mamurius, Numa, and the ancile. I mean, the more you know, right? But I came up empty, which makes me think that the legend is really obscure—well, compared to the world-famous myths about the Olympians and celebrity heroes, anyway. That doesn't make it any less real, though. Just a lot less known.

So the question is, if the original ancile exists, why isn't it in Mars's temple with the others? Or maybe it is. Maybe it just wasn't part of the M, and it's hanging on a different wall or locked away in a secret compartment or something. Only one way

to find out—pay another visit to my favorite god-crypt!

But not until tomorrow. Because tonight I'm going to my first gladiator exhibition! Janice scored us seats in the Colosseum's Blood Splash Zone. Scored me a cushion, too, because apparently those seats are hard as, well, the concrete they're made of.

The star of the show is the *murmillo* champion, a swarthy bit of beefcake named Ricardo. If the posters plastered around camp are accurate, he sword-fights wearing a teeny-tiny loincloth . . . and not much else. I'm praying *murmillo* is Latin for *he who wears undergarments beneath his loincloth*. Because if he falls down . . .

DAY XVI: *Games Gone Wild*

I'm no expert, but I don't think that's how gladiator games are supposed to go.

Last night's competition started out normally. The Colosseum was decked out with purple-and-gold banners and filled with cheering fans. The gladiators circled the arena, waving to the crowd before stopping at the praetors' box to salute Reyna and Frank. The praetors looked beat—dealing with oatmeal fiascos and faulty poop bags can tire even the strongest among us, apparently—but they smiled and waved back in acknowledgment.

Then the fights began. Swords clashed against

shields. Daggers stabbed into exposed flesh. The *laquearii* pinned arms with their lassoes, the retiarii wrapped heads with their weighted nets, and Ricardo the murmillo champ revealed that yes, he wears undergarments.

It was a fabulous performance that rivaled the best World Wrestling Entertainment matches. I know what I'm talking about, because Dad watches the WWE all the time. Made me a wee bit homesick thinking about him in his chair with the remote.

Thank goodness that gob of blood spattered me in the face when it did, or else I might have gotten all weepy. The Blood Splash Zone was out of wet wipes by then, so I excused myself to go down to the latrines to wash up.

Which is how I almost got caught in the flood.

Romans aren't known for their navy. A leaky rowboat and a couple tired-looking triremes are all

Camp Jupiter has for "ships." The naiads don't like it when we boat on the lake, so instead we flood the Colosseum and practice seafaring maneuvers (aka aimless drifting while trying to light cannons with wet matches) in ten feet of water in the arena.

Naval demonstrations weren't on last night's program, though. So why someone opened the Colosseum's floodgates is anybody's guess. Water gushed in, racing across the arena like a mini tidal wave and sweeping unsuspecting gladiators off their feet. Quick-thinking Colosseum workers saved the day by cranking open the drains. They saved the gladiators, too—at least the ones in heavy armor. If the water had gotten much deeper, there's no way could those guys have kept their heads above the surface.

It was mayhem in the Colosseum until a shout

cut through the noise. It was Praetor Reyna. I thought she was awe-inspiring (in a terrifying way) before. But seeing her standing above the receding water, Imperial gold dagger in hand, purple cape flapping in the wind, her warrior-fierce glare turning her dark eyes even darker . . . I mean, *wow*.

I'm glad I wasn't on the receiving end of her fury.

Not that anybody was, not last night, anyway. Her demands to know who had opened the floodgates were met with dead silence. Finally, she had no choice but to send us back to the barracks. She, Frank, and the centurions spent today hunting for the culprit, but with no luck.

Which sucks, because with all the weird stuff that's been going on, nerves are fraying in the ranks and people are eyeing one another with suspicion.

DAY XVII: *Target Practice*

All right, just what the *what* is going on?!

First the assembly horn wakes us up before dawn. We all stagger outside like well-trained zombies and form ranks. And then we get shot at! Not from enemies storming the earthen walls surrounding camp, but from our own watchtower crossbows! The weapons usually point outward. But as we lurched into position, they suddenly spun one-eighty degrees and—*chzzz! chzzz! chzzz!*—fired their arrows directly into camp.

Is that any way to start the day? No!

We would have fought back, but a) no one

was manning the crossbows, so there was no one to fight back against, and b) only the most seasoned legionnaires had thought to grab their weapons when the horn blared. As if things weren't confusing enough, startled Lares kept materializing to see what all the commotion was about—and then dematerializing when they saw what all the commotion was about. So brave, those ancient purple spirits.

The sentries finally got the crossbows under control, but only after the supply of arrows had run out. Thank the gods, no one was seriously hurt, just some scrapes and bruises and one twisted ankle (mine again—all hail the return of Claudia the Clumsy). I hobbled to the infirmary with the other casualties, only to learn the medics' stores of ambrosia and nectar were missing. So now the medical staff is working overtime making more of

both, and other essential supplies too. Pretty sure the unicorns' horns will be as thin as toothpicks by the time they're done being cheese-gratered.

Frank and Reyna have canceled our usual activities so they can launch a full-scale investigation into all the troubles going on at camp. And I'm going to do a little investigating myself . . . in the Temple of Mars Ultor.

Later . . .

CLOSED BY ORDER OF PRAETOR FRANK. That's the sign I found hanging on the massive iron door of Mars's temple. I've never heard of a temple being off-limits, but maybe Frank doesn't want whoever fired on us this morning to have access to Mars's weapon supply. When I couldn't go inside, I trooped all around the outside, looking for a window to peek in. Which is how I discovered Elon.

He was curled up in a nest of trash behind the temple, clutching what looked like a lava lamp filled with blobby green goop. On closer inspection—not that close, though, because I didn't want to wake him and because he still stank to high Olympus—the lava lamp was just an old glass soda bottle. The green stuff looked like swamp scum. Mmm, tasty.

I don't know if fauns are allowed on Temple Hill. But he looked so cute all snuggled up in that trash that I left him alone with his bottle.

Now I'm back in my bunk. I should be exhausted after playing Dodge the Arrow at the crack of dawn. But every time I close my eyes, I keep picturing that M shape made out of eleven shields. And I can't help wondering . . . where is number XII?

DAY XVIII:
Probably Not My Best Idea Yet

I'm an idiot! There's only one place the original ancile can be—the principia! It's the most secure building in camp. The elite praetorian guards protect the entrance to the headquarters. Get past them, and you have to deal with Reyna's vicious metal dogs, not to mention Reyna herself, who is even more ferocious. Frank seems pretty reasonable, but then again, he can turn into a lion and other intimidating creatures with claws and fangs. Plus there's the golden eagle standard mounted behind the praetors' desk, which Janice told me zaps laser beams from its eyes.

So basically, the ancile is out of my reach. Which is totally fine! There's no reason I need to see it! Except . . . yeah, I really want to see it. I want to know for sure that it's safe and sound in the principia. Too bad there's no way to sneak inside. Not even to take a quick peek.

Unless you happen to know about a secret ladder that leads from the aqueduct into the principia, that is. And if you're descended from the god of thieves . . . well, that should give you a big advantage in the sneaking-in department, right?

Later . . .

Oh, my gods. They think it's me. Frank and Reyna, they think *I'm* behind the troubles in camp!

I overheard them talking from my hiding place on the ladder below the iron grate. The oatmeal, the dead rats, the faulty poop sacks, the malfunctioning crossbows, even the Colosseum flood—as they pieced together the incidents like tiles in a mosaic, they thought they could see a picture forming.

A picture of *me*.

I eat oatmeal. I got into the principia with dead rats. I flew away with a bag of poop. I disappeared while on sentry duty and again during the gladiator games. In their eyes, the connections between me and the bizarre happenings are obvious.

The timeline of the problems points to me too, they said. Before I arrived, Camp Jupiter was running smoothly. Afterward, not so much. And then there was my strange behavior. Laughing hysterically at Frank after leaving Mars's temple. Holing up in the Fourth's latrine. Scribbling in a notebook. What was in that notebook, anyway? A list of future pranks? If so, they needed to confiscate it for the sake of the camp.

Then they dropped the final bomb: I was a legacy of Mercury, god of tricksters. Probatios have been known to act out to get their godly ancestors' attention. It was possible, probable even, that I was pulling increasingly elaborate—and dangerous—pranks to gain Mercury's blessing.

My heart was thudding so loudly by then I can't believe they didn't hear it. I wanted to scale the ladder and burst through the iron grate to tell them they were dead wrong. That I love being at Camp Jupiter and wouldn't do anything to jeopardize my place here or the safety of anyone who calls it home.

But I couldn't. Because there's no way they'd believe I was innocent. I mean, duh, I'd just made an unauthorized trek through the aqueducts to a secret entrance so I could spy inside the camp's headquarters for a hidden sacred item! And now I was eavesdropping on the legion's highest authorities. Couldn't look guiltier if I'd tried.

Reyna was ready to call me before the Senate then and there. But Frank, gods bless him, argued against confronting me, saying first they needed definite proof that I was behind the pranks. Reyna finally agreed, but I could tell she wasn't happy about it.

So now I'm hunched in my bunk, trying not to cry. Because it totally sucks that the praetors are suspicious of me. And it sucks that I can't let them know I know.

No, the only way to earn their trust is to prove my innocence. That means ferreting out the real culprit.

Reyna and Frank haven't been able to do that. But I'm holding mosaic tiles they don't know about: those mysterious messages and my dream about a runaway misfit. Unless MV shows up or the ancile falls in my lap, the messages are a dead end for now.

But I know just who to visit to dig up info on the girl of my dreams.

Day XIX:
How to Summon a God in Six Easy Steps

At a time when nearly all the gods have gone silent, there's one deity you can always get to appear by simply stepping over the line—the Pomerian Line, that is, the invisible boundary that encircles New Rome.

Sure enough, the second I put a sandaled toe over that borderline, Terminus popped up. Behind him was his comrade with arms, an adorable little girl named Julia who handles all matters in need of hands for him. When I told him I wanted to ask him some questions, not cross the line, he flashed me an exasperated look and vanished.

(Julia disappeared with him. How that happens is a mystery for another time.)

Undeterred, I took a step back and then a step forward.

Pop! Terminus and Julia reappeared. He took one look at me, yelled "You again?" and disappeared with an irritated huff (and with Julia).

I did the cha-cha to and fro again. "I can do this all day," I said when he materialized for the third time.

"Fine," he grumbled. "What do you want to talk about?"

"My dad," I answered. "And a little girl you didn't want to let into camp."

"You didn't let a little girl into camp?" Julia looked wounded. "Why?"

"Because reasons," he sniffed. "And I don't

know who your 'dad' is." (Julia supplied the fingers for his air quotes.)

I told him my dad was a centurion here about twenty-five years ago. When that didn't jog his memory, I mentioned the bleached-blond cowlick. He gave a snort of derision. "That boy became your father? My sympathies." He narrowed his eyes. "You don't look like him. You look like your mother."

My jaw dropped. A million questions flooded my brain, like, *How does he know my mother? Did my parents meet here? Was my mom a demigod or a legacy or what?*

But right then, my focus had to be on my dream girl. "Why did you refuse to let that girl into camp?"

Terminus's nose wrinkled. "Because she smelled like rotten eggs. Not her fault, I know, given who her godly parent was. But still . . ." He shuddered in distaste and vanished.

This time, I didn't summon him back. Instead, I returned to the barracks to think and write down

what I'd learned. If the praetors confiscate my journal, well, they'll see I was only trying to help.

Here's what I now know: The girl was a demigod, the daughter of a god or goddess associated with the smell of rotten eggs. The stench traveled with her, apparently, and was bad enough to make my dad, the legionnaires, and the aurae steer clear. Even gentle Hannibal couldn't stand it. The girl's parent wasn't an Olympian, because none of them have odoriferous attributes (although some say Juno stinks).

A minor deity, then. I've consulted my *ID the Deity* textbook and come up with a list of two possibilities: Cloacina, the goddess of the *cloaca maxima* sewer system, and Mefitis, goddess of noxious vapors that emanate from the earth.

There are a couple of Cloacina's kids here at camp, and I've never heard anyone complain about them smelling like rotten eggs or any other bad odor. So my denarius is on Mefitis.

DAY XX: *Well, That Stinks*

Question: Assuming the malodorous demigod was Mefitis's daughter, where would she go after she left Camp Jupiter?

Answer: Someplace where her out-of-control body odor wouldn't offend anyone.

A moment from my dream, when she tipped over the garbage can, points to one such place: the landfill. Can't do much better than that if you're looking to disguise your own stench. And I not only think she went there . . . I think she's *still* there.

She's the worker, the one who stared at me and Aquila. She saw us through the Mist, I'm sure of it. Which means she's a demigod. But if she's working and living at the dump, how can she be causing problems here? She can't be sneaking into camp, not if she's still as pungent as Terminus says she was. Someone would be sure to notice.

Maybe she has an accomplice in camp, though I don't know who would help her. From what I saw, she didn't have much to offer besides recyclables, garbage, and—

Oh. Oh, my gods, I am *such* an idiot. Because there is someone who would want that stuff. He even bragged about getting the pick of the litter.

Elon.

Later . . .

Message to whoever left me those notes: *Ego inveni MV*. Translation: I found MV.

But not Elon. He was gone when I returned to

Mars's temple to look for him. His trash nest was still there, though. Buried beneath it was the glass bottle of swamp scum. Except it wasn't swamp scum—it was swamp gas.

Mixed with the ghost of Mamurius Veturius.

The smell that came out of that bottle when I opened it . . . yee-gods. Poor Mamurius was a bilious shade of green when he stagger-floated out. Luckily, once he was in the fresh air again, he returned to his normal off-white and odor-free state. He regained his ghostly strength, too. Then he told me this story:

"Three weeks ago, I was floating around the forges when a young faun—Elon—ran up to me. Ran *through* me, actually, which I did not appreciate. 'Praetor Frank needs you!' he bleated urgently. 'Said to meet him in the Temple of Mars Ultor right away! Come on!'

"Frank was nowhere in sight when we arrived at the temple. Puzzled, I turned to question the faun. Suddenly, I was overcome by noxious fumes. When I came to, I was trapped inside that bottle with those same fumes. They sapped me of my strength, rendering me powerless to escape.

"The faun promised to free me. But only after I identified the original ancile from among the twelve mounted on the temple ceiling.

"I refused. I knew what would happen if that shield fell into the wrong hands. Better I be trapped in a bottle of stink forever than let the last outpost of ancient Rome fall." His vaporous shoulders slumped. "Alas, my refusal only delayed the eventual outcome."

His story ended then, and with a nod of gratitude for my part in saving him, he vanished. I'll check the forges later to make sure he's safe

and sound with his brother Blaise. I started down
the road out of Temple Hill too. Then I backtracked
and refilled Elon's bottle with scummy green water
scoured from the bowl on Neptune's altar. (You'd
think one of the Big Twelve would have something

better than that pathetic blue toolshed!) I put the bottle back in the trash nest where I'd found it. I hope it looks enough like Mamurius's toxic ghost to fool Elon.

Because if he figures out someone's onto him, Camp Jupiter is going to self-destruct for sure.

According to Mamurius's story, there should be twelve—XII—shields on the temple ceiling. But when I visited the god-crypt my second day of camp, there were only eleven. Add that fact to Mamurius's statement about the outcome, and I come up with one conclusion: I was wrong about the original ancile being in the principia. It was in Mars's temple with the others.

Emphasis on *was*.

So even without Mamurius's help, Elon somehow discovered which ancile was the original. By trial and error, maybe, sneaking them out of camp one at a time, waiting to see if anything happened, then moving on to the next one when nothing did.

Until finally . . . oatmeal. Or, to quote the voice inside the bathroom: *Mission accomplished.*

Well, there's a new mission now, called Ancile Recovery. Okay, that's a terrible name, but it's the best I've got until I think of a new one. And the name doesn't matter anyway.

Accomplishing the mission does.

DAY XXI: *Quest, Party of Three?*

Welp, Blaise is in love with me. Ha! JK. But he has sworn to help me with my mission—my *quest*, he says it should be called—because Mamurius told him all about how I freed him from the gassy bottle.

Having a demigod ally with mad forging skills fits right in with my plan to retrieve the ancile, actually. So does having Janice for a bestie.

I finally confided in her late last night. No surprise, she was more than ready to help save the camp. And New Rome, too, she pointed out, because if Camp Jupiter and the Twelfth Legion fell, the city wouldn't be far behind. I hadn't thought of that, but then, my dad is safe in his suburb. Her mom isn't.

Our only disagreement was over whether to tell the praetors what we'd discovered. After a hot debate (we were meeting in the forges because Mamurius wanted in on the plan and he refused to leave that workspace), I convinced them we should hold off going to Frank and Reyna until all the pieces of my plan were in place. That way, we could present the problem *and* the solution to them at the same time. When Blaise wondered aloud if my plan would even work, I pointed out that it includes stealth and booby traps, two of my specialties, so it was bound to succeed.

Agreement reached. Work commences after lunch.

• • •

After lunch . . .

Welp, I'm in love with Blaise. Ha! JK. But I am in awe of how fast he crafted the two-scutum garbage can I designed. It's based on the Janus strategy Janice came up with during deathball. I just added the hinge to connect the two shields on one side and the interior latch to hold the two together. Much easier than trying to keep them in place while shuffling back to back.

In addition to the Janus can, I appropriated— okay, *stole*—two sacks of deathballs, a retiarius net, and a laquearius lasso from the armory. I retrieved the plumbata I'd launched into the Colosseum stands during my first weapons practice and added it to the other supplies in the compostable poop bag. And finally, Janice, Blaise, and I figured out how to bottle Bombilo's bakery smell. (I suppose I should thank Elon for proving it's possible to capture odors that way. And I will . . . riiiight after I pin him to the wall with my plumbata.)

I'm on sentry duty tonight, so after dinner I'll stash the bag by the aviary on my way to the watchtower.

After dinner . . .

Welp, Elon is in love with Mefitis's smelly daughter. Ha! JK. But he *is* terrified of Mimi—that's the demigod's name: Mimi. I learned all these facts by eavesdropping on their conversation inside the bathroom. I suspect she doesn't actually show up in there but somehow speaks through the toilet—tapping into the noxious vapors that collect there, or some such. That's a lovely thought. . . .

Anyway, after leaving the supply sack hidden at the aviary, I took off for sentry duty. I didn't want to repeat my previous bladder blunder, so I veered to the bathroom for a quick pit stop.

The same voices were murmuring inside again. I ducked behind a tree to listen in on their cozy toilet-side chat. And was silently freaked out by what I heard.

The day after tomorrow, Mimi is scheduled to work alone at the landfill's car crusher. She's going to bring the ancile . . . and pulverize it in the machine.

I wasn't the only one pushing the panic button at that news. I thought Elon was going to bleat himself hoarse. With good reason. He's a mythical creature born of ancient Rome. If ancient Rome ceases to exist, well, my guess is so does he and all his kind. Not sure he thought that one through when he signed on with Mimi. Or the fact that other species will vanish, too, like the friendly dog-headed *cynocephali*, rowdy centaurs, naiads and dryads, and—OMG! Bombilo, the two-headed baker! Noooooo!

The eradication of ancient Roman beings might not stop with mythical creatures, either. Without the lingering aura of ancient Rome to bolster them, gods and goddesses could fade away too. The Olympians will probably be fine—that lot seems to

survive everything thrown at them. It's the minor deities I'm afraid for. Janice says some of them are already so lost to the modern world's memory that they're hanging on by a thread. As usual, when tragedy strikes, the powerless and disenfranchised are the ones who suffer most.

So that seals it. We *will* succeed in retrieving the ancile if it's the last thing we do! We must, we can, we will!

DAY XXII: *Not. So. Fast.*

Oh, gods. I'm in deep, deep trouble. Like, way far down in Tartarus town deep.

My mind was spinning when I left the bathroom last night. Every nerve in my body screamed, *DO SOMETHING!* So I found (aka bribed) someone to take my sentry duty and returned to the aviary. My idea? Fly Aquila on a reconnaissance mission over the dump. Specifically, to the car crusher, where I'd look for a way to shut it down or blow it up—okay, not blow it up, but at least clog its works for a few days to buy Janice, Blaise, and me some time to finesse our plan.

Aquila was dozing up in her treetop nest when I slipped inside the eagle enclosure. I tried throwing pebbles at her to wake her up, but as my pitiful plumbata toss demonstrated during weapons practice, my arm and my aim aren't very good. So I started to climb. I got about halfway up when I heard a voice that chilled me to the bone.

"Not. So. Fast."

It was Reyna. I learned later that she'd been following me ever since dinner. Watching and waiting to catch me doing something I shouldn't be doing. Like ditching sentry duty and shinnying up a tree to steal a giant eagle for a joy ride.

I slowly climbed down, fully expecting praetorian guards to clap me in irons when I reached the ground. But Reyna was alone. Alone and very angry.

"Explain yourself, probatio. And know that

if I don't like what I hear, I will drag you before the Senate in chains."

I don't know what possessed me, I really don't. But instead of telling her the full story then and there, I said, "Not here. In the principia. Just you, me, and Praetor Frank." I swallowed hard. "And your dogs."

She blinked in surprise. Aurum and Argentum have a special talent: they can sense when someone is lying. (Their other special talent is eating jelly beans.) If their lie detectors go off, they attack the liar. So basically, I'd be a dead probatio if I told even one little fib.

Reyna agreed and ordered me confined to my

bunk while she went to look for Frank. When she finds him, she'll summon me. And then I talk. May the gods bless me with a silver and truthful tongue.

If not . . . Great-Granddad, if you're listening, get this message to my dad, okay? "I love you. And I tried."

DAY XXIII: *Going to the Dogs*

I'm still alive! Well, obviously.

It wasn't easy telling the praetors about the ancile, Elon, Mimi, and the messages, not with those dogs staring at me hungrily, Reyna's lips getting tighter and tighter, and Frank looking embarrassed and murmuring, "I never even noticed those shields in Dad's temple. Never heard of the ancile legend, either." I got through it, though. Thought I was home free. Then Frank leaned over the desk and asked one question: "Does anyone else know about this?"

My throat closed up with fear. No way was

I going to pull Janice and Blaise into this. Or Mamurius, for that matter. I already felt terrible for throwing Elon under the chariot. I mean, sure, the faun has an annoying habit of referring to himself in the third person, and his weakness for trash has brought us to the brink of destruction. Put those things aside, though, and he's just a scared little kid with a soda-tab necklace.

When I hesitated, Frank repeated his question. I had to choose then: rope my friends into this mess with me, or lie and die.

Reyna saved me. Even as I write those words, I still can't believe it. But she did. She held up her hand to signal me to stay quiet, then called out, "Bring them in!"

Praetorian guards led Janice and Blaise inside. Mamurius drifted in after them. Frank explained that the three had come to him when they heard I had been confined to my bunk. (Word gets around fast about that sort of stuff, apparently.) They'd told him all they knew before I got there. They'd also outlined the plan I had proposed for dealing with Mimi and getting the ancile back.

While Frank was talking, Reyna studied me. And continued to study me after he finished. Then, to my astonishment, she smiled. "Your loyalty to your friends is admirable, Claudia. Your forthright truthfulness, too, though it's a little late in coming."

She sat back and steepled her fingers. "Now then. About your plan to deal with Mimi . . . I have one change to make to it." She nodded toward Frank. "Instead of endangering Aquila, Frank will fly you and your supplies to the landfill. Agreed?"

The idea of boarding Air Praetor wasn't hugely appealing—it still isn't—but I was in no position to argue, and she was in no mood to debate. "Agreed."

So now I'm back in my bunk yet again. My fellow legionnaires are whispering about me, because they think I'm still in trouble. But I'm just waiting for nightfall and praying that the first part of my plan is going off without a hitch.

Because we have just one shot to get this right. If we fail, the ancile is history . . . and so are Camp Jupiter, New Rome, and all ancient Roman creatures great and small. If we succeed, though, we'll get in, get out, and be back in time for breakfast.

For the sake of the Twelfth Legion Fulminata, I hope it's not oatmeal.

DAY XXIV:
Exploding Poop Bags and Spritz Bottles, Anyone?

Right. Here's how it was *supposed* to go yesterday:

Frank the giant eagle was to transport a poop-free compostable garbage bag filled with deathballs, the Janus can, the retiarius net, and the laquearius lasso to the landfill.

What actually happened:

Frank the giant eagle crash-landed while transporting what he thought was a poop-free compostable garbage bag filled with the aforementioned items, but which upon impact was discovered to contain nothing but poop. And a single deathball, which Hannibal's handler suspects Hannibal ingested by mistake. Ick.

While Frank visited the infirmary to get his broken wing, um, arm repaired, Blaise, Janice, and I scrapped our original concept and improvised. Under cover of darkness and armed with spritz bottles of Bombilo's Café Scent, we lugged the deathballs, the Janus can, and the other weapons through secret tunnels, over the hills, and through the woods to the landfill. (No one thought to tell us that Reyna had access to a truck. Not that any of us can drive . . . but still.) I'd dreaded the hike, because I knew the others would look to me, the descendant of the god of travelers, to steer them in the right direction, and frankly, after my aqueduct wanderings, I wasn't sure I was up to the task.

Fortunately, we got an unexpected guide for our journey: Elon.

Mamurius had tracked down the faun soon after leaving the principia. He promised/threatened to make whatever remained of Elon's life a living Underworld if he didn't help us. Elon was more than happy to lend a hoof since it meant stopping Mimi. He knew the way, too, since he'd been traveling to and from the landfill to feast on trash for days. As an added bonus, as we hiked, we convinced him to stop referring to himself in the third person. Win-win!

When we reached the edge of the landfill, we changed into our disguises—hard hats and bright yellow safety vests. If anyone questioned us, we'd say we were workers on the night shift. No clue if the landfill has a night shift, but it was the best we could come up with on short notice. We sent Elon back to camp with a message for the praetors and a spare bottle of Bombilo's—which he was happily drinking when I looked back—then crept over mountains of wet, slimy garbage toward Mimi's trailer.

Worst. Hike. Ever.

We reached the trailer without incident. As quickly and quietly as we could, we went to work setting the booby traps. We hung the weighted net over the doorway and planted a sea of deathballs on the steps. We dug a trench in the trash just beyond the stairs and built an arch made of recyclables above it. When Janice had attached the lasso to the keystone, we took up our positions: Janice and Blaise tucked inside the protection of the Janus can with the rope and me on the trailer roof above the net.

I gave Blaise the go-ahead nod. He threw a rock at the trailer door and quickly crouched back down inside the can.

I held my breath. Moments passed. Then a light came on inside the trailer. The door opened. A woman emerged. A woman, and the most *unbelievable* stench, like the inside of an old milk carton mixed with moldering gym clothes all doused in skunk spray.

Ladies and gentlemen, Mimi had left the building.

It was time to act. I released the net. It dropped over Mimi's head and wrapped her up like a used Christmas tree. She let out a howl and lurched onto the steps. Her feet hit the deathballs. She skated, slipped, and sprawled straight into the trench. Janice yanked the pull rope. The keystone popped free, and in one glorious cascade, the arch and all the trash piled up around it fell on top of Mimi.

I swung from the roof through the open door

into the trailer. I tore through closets and looked under the bed. Nothing. I pulled open drawers and checked the shower stall. Still nothing. I spun in circles, desperately searching for the ancile or something, *anything*, that would point to its whereabouts.

I almost missed it. Lying horizontal at waist height and covered by a length of purple fabric, it looked like an ironing board. But when I whisked the fabric away, there it was. The missing shield.

I snatched it up—carefully—and raced outside to find Janice and Blaise madly spritzing a moving mound of garbage with Bombilo's Café Scent. That mouthwatering odor held her at bay just long enough for reinforcements to reach us. Aquila, Frank, and another giant eagle swooped in, caught us in their talons, and flew us off into the moonlight.

Camp Jupiter had never looked so splendid. And the baths . . . oh. Pure heaven.

DAY XXV: *The End (JK!)*

I've been thinking a lot about secrets. Me and my messages and dream. The identity of the one true ancile. Elon's wackadoodle relationship with Mimi. Would our situation have gotten so out of control if people had opened up and shared what they knew sooner? Maybe.

But mostly, I've been thinking about a new secret I learned today.

I was in New Rome, on my way to the library, where a new-but-old paving stone was going to be laid. The name etched on the paver? Mamurius Veturius. He wasn't recognized as a hero in his lifetime, but he sure helped save the day in ours.

I was killing some time before the ceremony by wandering the streets. Janice had offered to go with me. Blaise, too—he turned red as a forge fire when he mumbled it, which makes me wonder if maybe he *is* in love with me after all. Well. Plenty of time for that sort of thing now that Camp Jupiter is safe.

I told them both thanks, but no thanks. I wanted to explore New Rome on my own this time. To drink in the sights, sounds, and yep, the smells, without any distractions. To imagine my father walking these same cobblestone streets. I had no route in mind—I just let my feet take me where they would.

They steered me to a place I'd never been to before, yet it was as familiar as the back of my hand. A doorway to a modest home tucked on a side street. There was nothing unusual about it—it looked just like every other front door on that street.

Except it was open. And leaning against the frame was a woman with dark wavy hair. Like mine. Dark eyes. Like mine. A big nose. Like mine. Her hand drifted to her stomach and rested there. And then she smiled at me.

"Hello, Claudia." Her voice was soft and high with just the hint of a squeak.

I froze in my tracks, speechless. Then I cleared my throat. "M-Mom?"

Her smile widened. She pushed off the doorframe and moved toward me. Took my hands in hers. "My name is Cardea—Cardi, to you and your father."

"The goddess of thresholds and hinges," I murmured. (Thank you, ID the Deity class!)

She nodded. "I have been allowed to contact you in this form because of what you did to save our world. Without you and your friends . . . well, we 'minor' deities [Julia would have been proud of my mom's mad air-quote skills] might not be here."

"In this form," I repeated. "Meaning . . . you've contacted me in other ways?" I gave myself a mental head slap. "The messages. They were from

you, not Great-Granddad?"

She seesawed her hand in a *maybe/maybe not* gesture. "I wrote them, yes. But I couldn't have delivered them, not without his help."

I nodded my understanding, remembering what Leila had said about the recent problems with communications. Still . . . "If you knew what was going on, with the ancile and everything, why didn't you or the other gods intervene to stop Mimi?"

Her lovely face clouded over. "Because reasons," she said softly.

(Reyna told me later that gods and goddesses don't appreciate it when other deities muck about in their children's affairs. Doesn't stop them from doing it all the time, of course. And at least my mom had done what she could to help.)

Cardea's form started to flicker then. "My time here is almost up. Hold out your arm, quickly." I did as she requested. "This is supposed to be done in the Forum before the Senate and the Legion, but they're a little busy right now, so . . ." She met my eyes apologetically. "Close your eyes. This might hurt."

It *did* hurt. A lot, in fact. A searing pain like when you brush against a hot stove, only a billion times worse. It was over quickly, though. And when I opened my eyes, I saw what had caused the burning sensation. There were now four tattoos on my forearm: a hinge, a caduceus, a single stripe, and the letters SPQR.

Mom traced her fingers over the images, a touch so featherlight I wouldn't have felt it if I hadn't seen her hand. And then her form faded away, and I was left with just her soft whisper in my ear. *"Senatus Populusque Romanus!"*

I saluted the sky. "SPQR, Mom! SPQR forever!"

BERKELEY
FIELD of MARS
VIA PRINCIPALIS
BATHS
DECUMANIAN GATE
PRAETORIAN GATE
CALDECOTT TUNNEL
PRINCIPIA
VIA PRAETORIA
BARRACKS
MESS
FIFTH COHORT
N
W
E
S
LITTLE TIBER
OAKLAND HILLS

BERKELEY HILLS
AQUEDUCT
NEW ROME
POMERIAN LINE
COLOSSEUM
SENATE HOUSE
FORUM
CIRCUS MAXIMUS
THE LAKE
MOUNT DIABLO
JUPITER OPTIMUS MAXIMUS
PLUTO
BELLONA
TEMPLE HILL
MARS ULTOR
CAMP JUPITER

GLOSSARY

ancile (*ancilia*, pl.) an ornate and cello-shaped shield; one of twelve sacred shields kept in the Temple of Mars

aqueduct a structure built to ferry water from a distant source

aquila Latin for *eagle*

Athena the Greek goddess of wisdom. Roman form: Minerva

aura (*aurae*, pl.) wind spirit

Bellona a Roman goddess of war; daughter of Jupiter and Juno

caduceus a herald's staff carried by Mercury, with a pair of wings at the top and snakes entwined around the shaft

Camp Jupiter the training ground for Roman

demigods, located in California, between the Oakland Hills and the Berkeley Hills

Cardea Roman goddess of the hinge

centaur a being with the torso and head of a man and the body of a horse

centurion an officer in the Roman army

Claudius Roman emperor from 41 to 54 CE

cloaca maxima Latin for *greatest sewer*

Cloacina the Roman goddess who presided over the cloaca maxima

cohort a group of legionnaires

Colosseum an elliptical amphitheater built for gladiator fights, monster simulations, and mock naval battles

cynocephalus (*cynocephali*, pl.) a being with a human body and a dog's head

Decumanian Gate Camp Jupiter's western entrance

denarius (denarii, pl.) a unit of Roman currency

dryad a spirit (usually female) associated with a certain tree

faun a Roman forest god, part goat and part man. Greek form: satyr

Field of Mars part battlefield, part party zone, the place where drills and war games are held at Camp Jupiter

Forum the center of life in New Rome; a plaza with statues and fountains that is lined with shops and nighttime entertainment venues

fulminata Latin for *armed with lightning*; a Roman legion under Julius Caesar whose emblem was a   lightning bolt (*fulmen*)

Gaea the Greek earth goddess; wife of Ouranos; mother of the Titans, giants, Cyclopes, and other monsters. Roman form: Terra

galea Latin for *helmet*

gladiator a person trained to fight with particular weapons in an arena

gladius a stabbing sword; the primary weapon of Roman foot soldiers

greaves shin armor

Imperial gold a rare metal deadly to monsters, consecrated at the Pantheon; its existence was a closely guarded secret of the emperors

invenient Latin for *find*

Janus the Roman god of doorways, transitions, beginnings, and endings

Juno the Roman goddess of marriage; Jupiter's wife and sister; Apollo's stepmother. Greek form: Hera

Jupiter the Roman god of the sky and king of the gods. Greek form: Zeus

laquearius (*laquearii*, pl.) Latin for *snarer*; a gladiator who fought with a lasso in one hand and a sword in the other

Lar (*Lares*, pl.) Roman house gods

legion a unit of soldiers in the Roman army

legionnaire a member of the Roman army

Little Tiber named after the Tiber River of Rome, the smallest river that forms the barrier of Camp Jupiter

Lupa the wolf goddess, guardian spirit of Rome

Mamurius Veturius master craftsman to King Numa, who instructed him to make eleven identical copies of the ancile

manubalista a Roman heavy crossbow

Mars Ultor the Avenger, another name for the Roman god of war

Mefitis the Roman goddess of noxious vapors that emanate from the earth

Mercury the Roman god of travelers; guide to spirits of the dead; god of communication. Greek form: Hermes

Mist a magical force that prevents mortals from seeing gods, mythical creatures, and supernatural occurrences by replacing them with things the human mind can comprehend

murmillo the oldest gladiator fighting style, in which the gladius sword is the primary weapon

naiad a female water spirit

Neptune the Roman god of the sea. Greek form: Poseidon

New Rome both the valley in which Camp Jupiter is located and a city—a smaller, modern version of the ancient imperial city—where Roman demigods can go to live in peace, study, and retire

Numa the king who took the throne after Rome's founder, Romulus, died

oculus the round skylight in the center of a domed ceiling

pilum a javelin

plumbata a throwing dart

Pluto the Roman god of death and ruler of the Underworld. Greek form: Hades

Pomerian Line the invisible boundary that encircles New Rome

praetor an elected Roman magistrate and commander of the army

praetorian guard a unit of elite Roman soldiers in the Imperial Roman Army

principia the military headquarters for the praetors at Camp Jupiter

probatio the rank assigned to new members of the legion at Camp Jupiter

pugio a dagger

purgamentorum derelinquere caeno Latin for *sewage sludge*

retiarius (*retiarii*, pl.) a gladiator who fights with a net and a trident or dagger

Romulus a demigod son of Mars, twin brother of Remus; the first king of Rome, who founded the city in 753 BCE

scutum a large curved shield

Senate a council of ten representatives elected from the legion at Camp Jupiter

SPQR an abbreviation for *Senatus Populusque Romanus* (Senate and People of Rome)

Temple Hill the site just outside the city limits of New Rome where the temples to all the gods are located

Terminus the Roman god of boundaries

testudo a tortoise battle formation in which legionnaires put their shields together to form a barrier

trireme a Greek warship, having three tiers of oars on each side

Via Praetoria the main road into Camp Jupiter

that runs from the barracks to the headquarters

Vulcan the Roman god of fire, including volcanic, and of crafts and blacksmithing. Greek form: Hephaestus

Not ready to leave Camp Jupiter?

Read the first chapter of

The Trials of Apollo Book 4:
The Tyrant's Tomb

1

There is no food here
Meg ate all the Swedish Fish
Please get off my hearse

I BELIEVE IN RETURNING DEAD BODIES.

It seems like a simple courtesy, doesn't it? A warrior dies, you should do what you can to get their body back to their people for funerary rites. Maybe I'm old-fashioned. (I *am* over four thousand years old.) But I find it rude not to properly dispose of corpses.

Achilles during the Trojan War, for instance. *Total* pig. He chariot-dragged the body of the Trojan champion Hector around the walls of the city for days. Finally I convinced Zeus to pressure the big bully into returning Hector's body to his parents so he could have a decent burial. I mean, *come on.* Have a little respect for the people you slaughter.

Then there was Oliver Cromwell's corpse. I wasn't a fan of the man, but please. First, the English bury him with honors. Then they decide they hate him, so they dig him up and "execute" his body. Then his head falls off the pike where it's been impaled for decades and gets passed around from collector to collector for almost three centuries like a disgusting souvenir snow globe. Finally, in 1960,

I whispered in the ears of some influential people, *Enough, already. I am the god Apollo, and I order you to bury that thing. You're grossing me out.*

When it came to Jason Grace, my fallen friend and half brother, I wasn't going to leave anything to chance. I would personally escort his coffin to Camp Jupiter and see him off with full honors.

That turned out to be a good call. What with the ghouls attacking us and everything.

Sunset turned San Francisco Bay into a cauldron of molten copper as our private plane landed at Oakland Airport. I say *our* private plane; the chartered trip was actually a parting gift from our friend Piper McLean and her movie star father. (Everyone should have at least one friend with a movie star parent.)

Waiting for us beside the runway was another surprise the McLeans must have arranged: a gleaming black hearse.

Meg McCaffrey and I stretched our legs on the tarmac while the ground crew somberly removed Jason's coffin from the Cessna's storage bay. The polished mahogany box seemed to glow in the evening light. Its brass fixtures glinted red. I hated how beautiful it was. Death shouldn't be beautiful.

The crew loaded it into the hearse, then transferred our luggage to the backseat. We didn't have much: Meg's backpack and mine, my bow and quiver and ukulele, and a couple of sketchbooks and a poster-board diorama we'd inherited from Jason.

I signed some paperwork, accepted the flight crew's

condolences, then shook hands with a nice undertaker who handed me the keys to the hearse and walked away.

I stared at the keys, then at Meg McCaffrey, who was chewing the head off a Swedish Fish. The plane had been stocked with half a dozen tins of the squishy red candy. Not anymore. Meg had single-handedly brought the Swedish Fish ecosystem to the brink of collapse.

"I'm supposed to drive?" I wondered. "Is this a rental hearse? I'm pretty sure my New York junior driver's license doesn't cover this."

Meg shrugged. During our flight, she'd insisted on sprawling on the Cessna's sofa, so her dark pageboy haircut was flattened against the side of her head. One rhinestone-studded point of her cat-eye glasses poked through her hair like a disco shark fin.

The rest of her outfit was equally disreputable: floppy red high-tops, threadbare yellow leggings, and the well-loved knee-length green frock she'd gotten from Percy Jackson's mother. By *well-loved*, I mean the frock had been through so many battles, been washed and mended so many times, it looked less like a piece of clothing and more like a deflated hot-air balloon. Around Meg's waist was the pièce de résistance: her multi-pocketed gardening belt, because children of Demeter never leave home without one.

"I don't have a driver's license," she said, as if I needed a reminder that my life was presently being controlled by a twelve-year-old. "I call shotgun."

"Calling shotgun" didn't seem appropriate for a hearse. Nevertheless, Meg skipped to the passenger's side and climbed in. I got behind the wheel. Soon we were out of the airport and cruising north on I-880 in our rented black grief-mobile.

Ah, the Bay Area . . . I'd spent some happy times here. The vast misshapen geographic bowl was jam-packed with interesting people and places. I loved the green-and-golden hills, the fog-swept coastline, the glowing lacework of bridges, and the crazy zigzag of neighborhoods shouldered up against one another like subway passengers at rush hour.

Back in the 1950s, I played with Dizzy Gillespie at Bop City in the Fillmore. During the Summer of Love, I hosted an impromptu jam session in Golden Gate Park with the Grateful Dead. (Lovely bunch of guys, but did they *really* need those fifteen-minute-long solos?) In the 1980s, I hung out in Oakland with Stan Burrell—otherwise known as MC Hammer—as he pioneered pop rap. I can't claim credit for Stan's music, but I *did* advise him on his fashion choices. Those gold lamé parachute pants? My idea. You're welcome, fashionistas.

Most of the Bay Area brought back good memories. But as I drove, I couldn't help glancing to the northwest—toward Marin County and the dark peak of Mount Tamalpais. We gods knew the place as Mount Othrys, seat of the Titans. Even though our ancient enemies had been cast down, their palace destroyed, I could still feel the evil pull of the place—like a magnet trying to extract the iron from my now-mortal blood.

I did my best to shake the feeling. We had other problems to deal with. Besides, we were going to Camp Jupiter—friendly territory on this side of the bay. I had Meg for backup. I was driving a hearse. What could possibly go wrong?

The Nimitz Freeway snaked through the East Bay flatlands, past warehouses and docklands, strip malls and rows of dilapidated bungalows. To our right rose downtown Oakland, its small cluster of high-rises facing off against its cooler neighbor San Francisco across the bay as if to proclaim, *We are Oakland! We exist, too!*

Meg reclined in her seat, propped her red high-tops up on the dashboard, and cracked open her window.

"I like this place," she decided.

"We just got here," I said. "What is it you like? The abandoned warehouses? That sign for Bo's Chicken 'N' Waffles?"

"Nature."

"Concrete counts as nature?"

"There's trees, too. Plants flowering. Moisture in the air. The eucalyptus smells good. It's not like . . ."

She didn't need to finish her sentence. Our time in Southern California had been marked by scorching temperatures, extreme drought, and raging wildfires—all thanks to the magical Burning Maze controlled by Caligula and his hate-crazed sorceress bestie, Medea. The Bay Area wasn't experiencing any of those problems. Not at the moment, anyway.

We'd killed Medea. We'd extinguished the Burning Maze. We'd freed the Erythraean Sibyl and brought relief to the mortals and withering nature spirits of Southern California.

But Caligula was still very much alive. He and his co-emperors in the Triumvirate were still intent on controlling all means of prophecy, taking over the world, and writing the future in their own sadistic image. Right now, Caligula's fleet of evil luxury yachts was making its way toward San Francisco to attack Camp Jupiter. I could only imagine what sort of hellish destruction the emperor would rain down on Oakland and Bo's Chicken 'N' Waffles.

Even if we somehow managed to defeat the Triumvirate, there was still that greatest Oracle, Delphi, under the control of my old nemesis Python. How I could defeat him in my present form as a sixteen-year-old weakling, I had no idea.

But, hey. Except for that, everything was fine. The eucalyptus smelled nice.

Traffic slowed at the I-580 interchange. Apparently, California drivers didn't follow that custom of yielding to hearses out of respect. Perhaps they figured at least one of our passengers was already dead, so we weren't in a hurry.

Meg toyed with her window control, raising and lowering the glass. *Reeee. Reeee. Reeee.*

"You know how to get to Camp Jupiter?" she asked.

"Of course."

"'Cause you said that about Camp Half-Blood."

"We got there! Eventually."

"Frozen and half-dead."

"Look, the entrance to camp is right over there." I waved vaguely at the Oakland Hills. "There's a secret passage in the Caldecott Tunnel or something."

"Or something?"

"Well, I haven't actually ever *driven* to Camp Jupiter," I admitted. "Usually I descend from the heavens in my glorious sun chariot. But I know the Caldecott Tunnel is the main entrance. There's probably a sign. Perhaps a *demigods only* lane."

Meg peered at me over the top of her glasses. "You're the dumbest god ever." She raised her window with a final *reeee SHLOOMP!*—a sound that reminded me uncomfortably of a guillotine blade.

We turned northeast onto Highway 24. The congestion eased as the hills loomed closer. The elevated lanes soared past neighborhoods of winding streets and tall conifers, white stucco houses clinging to the sides of grassy ravines.

A road sign promised CALDECOTT TUNNEL ENTRANCE, 2 MI. That should have comforted me. Soon, we'd pass through the borders of Camp Jupiter into a heavily guarded, magically camouflaged valley where an entire Roman legion could shield me from my worries, at least for a while.

Why, then, were the hairs on the back of my neck quivering like sea worms?

Something was wrong. It dawned on me that the uneasiness I'd felt since we landed might not be the distant threat of Caligula, or the old Titan base on Mount Tamalpais, but something more immediate . . . something malevolent, and getting closer.

I glanced in the rearview mirror. Through the back window's gauzy curtains, I saw nothing but traffic. But then, in the polished surface of Jason's coffin lid, I caught the reflection of movement from a dark shape outside—as if a human-size object had just flown past the hearse.

"Oh, Meg?" I tried to keep my voice even. "Do you see anything unusual behind us?"

"Unusual like what?"

THUMP.

The hearse lurched as if we'd been hitched to a trailer full of scrap metal. Above my head, two foot-shaped impressions appeared in the upholstered ceiling.

"Something just landed on the roof," Meg deduced.

"Thank you, Sherlock McCaffrey! Can you get it off?"

"Me? How?"

That was an annoyingly fair question. Meg could turn the rings on her middle fingers into wicked gold swords, but if she summoned them in close quarters, like the interior of the hearse, she a) wouldn't have room to wield them, and b) might end up impaling me and/or herself.

CREAK. CREAK. The footprint impressions deepened as the thing adjusted its weight like a surfer on a board. It must have been immensely heavy to sink into the metal roof.

A whimper bubbled in my throat. My hands trembled on the steering wheel. I yearned for my bow and quiver in the backseat, but I couldn't have used them. DWSPW, driving while shooting projectile weapons, is a big no-no, kids.

"Maybe you can open the window," I said to Meg. "Lean out and tell it to go away."

"Um, no." (Gods, she was stubborn.) "What if you try to shake it off?"

Before I could explain that this was a terrible idea while traveling fifty miles an hour on a highway, I heard a sound like a pop-top aluminum can opening—the crisp, pneumatic hiss of air through metal. A claw punctured the ceiling—a grimy white talon the size of a drill bit. Then another. And another. And another, until the upholstery was studded with ten pointy white spikes—just the right number for two very large hands.

"Meg?" I yelped. "Could you—?"

I don't know how I might have finished that sentence. *Protect me? Kill that thing? Check in the back to see if I have any spare undies?*

I was rudely interrupted by the creature ripping open our roof like we were a birthday present.

Staring down at me through the ragged hole was a withered, ghoulish humanoid, its blue-black hide glistening like the skin of a housefly, its eyes filmy white orbs, its bared teeth dripping saliva. Around its torso fluttered a loincloth of greasy black feathers. The smell coming off it was more putrid than any dumpster—and believe me, I'd fallen into a few.

"FOOD!" it howled.

"Kill it!" I yelled at Meg.

"Swerve!" she countered.

One of the many annoying things about being incarcerated in my puny mortal body: I was Meg McCaffrey's servant. I was bound to obey her direct commands. So when she yelled "Swerve," I yanked the steering wheel hard to the right. The hearse handled beautifully. It careened across three lanes of traffic, barreled straight through the guardrail, and plummeted into the canyon below.

Turn the page to see who's who
in your favorite Riordan series

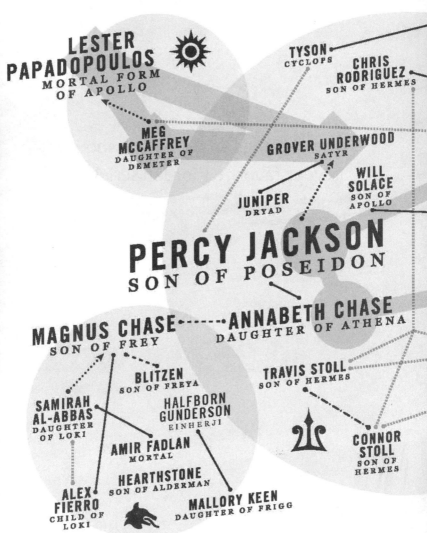

READ **RIORDAN**

DEMIGOD MAP

RELATIONS & SHIPS

LESTER PAPADOPOULOS
MORTAL FORM OF APOLLO

TYSON
CYCLOPS

CHRIS RODRIGUEZ
SON OF HERMES

MEG MCCAFFREY
DAUGHTER OF DEMETER

GROVER UNDERWOOD
SATYR

WILL SOLACE
SON OF APOLLO

JUNIPER
DRYAD

PERCY JACKSON
SON OF POSEIDON

ANNABETH CHASE
DAUGHTER OF ATHENA

MAGNUS CHASE
SON OF FREY

BLITZEN
SON OF FREYA

TRAVIS STOLL
SON OF HERMES

SAMIRAH AL-ABBAS
DAUGHTER OF LOKI

HALFBORN GUNDERSON
EINHERJI

AMIR FADLAN
MORTAL

CONNOR STOLL
SON OF HERMES

HEARTHSTONE
SON OF ALDERMAN

ALEX FIERRO
CHILD OF LOKI

MALLORY KEEN
DAUGHTER OF FRIGG

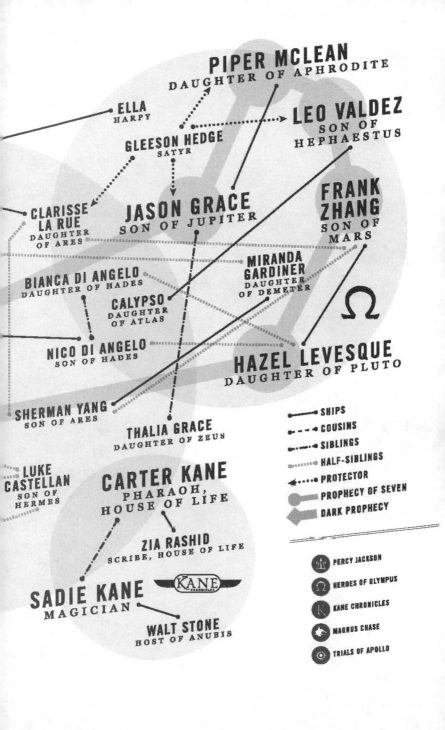

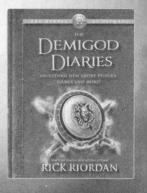

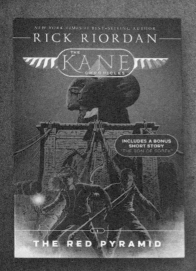

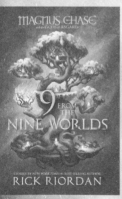
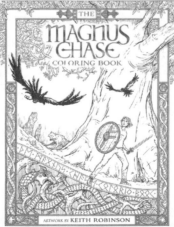

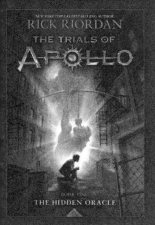

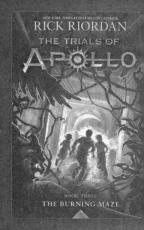
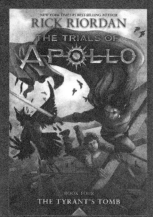
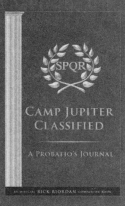

Also by Rick Riordan

PERCY JACKSON AND THE OLYMPIANS
Book One: *The Lightning Thief*
Book Two: *The Sea of Monsters*
Book Three: *The Titan's Curse*
Book Four: *The Battle of the Labyrinth*
Book Five: *The Last Olympian*
The Demigod Files
The Lightning Thief: The Graphic Novel
The Sea of Monsters: The Graphic Novel
The Titan's Curse: The Graphic Novel
The Battle of the Labyrinth: The Graphic Novel
The Last Olympian: The Graphic Novel
Percy Jackson's Greek Gods
Percy Jackson's Greek Heroes
From Percy Jackson: Camp Half-Blood Confidential

THE KANE CHRONICLES
Book One: *The Red Pyramid*
Book Two: *The Throne of Fire*
Book Three: *The Serpent's Shadow*
The Red Pyramid: The Graphic Novel
The Throne of Fire: The Graphic Novel
The Serpent's Shadow: The Graphic Novel
From the Kane Chronicles: Brooklyn House Magician's Manual

ABOUT THE AUTHOR

RICK RIORDAN, dubbed "storyteller of the gods" by *Publishers Weekly*, is the author of five *New York Times* #1 best-selling middle grade series with millions of copies sold throughout the world: Percy Jackson and the Olympians, the Heroes of Olympus, and the Trials of Apollo, based on Greek and Roman mythology; the Kane Chronicles, based on Egyptian mythology; and Magnus Chase and the Gods of Asgard, based on Norse mythology. Rick collaborated with illustrator John Rocco on two best-selling collections of Greek myths for the whole family: *Percy Jackson's Greek Gods* and *Percy Jackson's Greek Heroes*. Rick is also the publisher of an imprint at Disney Hyperion, Rick Riordan Presents, dedicated to finding other authors of highly entertaining fiction based on world cultures and mythologies. He lives in Boston, Massachusetts, with his wife and two sons. Follow him on Twitter @camphalfblood. To learn more about him and his books, visit www.RickRiordan.com.